The Wizlets

The Magic
Waste-Goat

The Wizlets
The Magic Waste-Goat

Jamie Rix

Illustrated by Sue Heap

Scholastic Children's Books,
Commonwealth House, 1–19 New Oxford Street,
London WC1A 1NU, UK
a division of Scholastic Ltd
London ~ New York ~ Toronto ~ Sydney ~ Auckland
Mexico City ~ New Delhi ~ Hong Kong

First published by Scholastic Ltd, 1999

ISBN 0 590 11354 2

Typeset by DP Photosetting, Aylesbury, Bucks
Printed by Mackays of Chatham plc, Chatham, Kent

10 9 8 7 6 5 4 3 2 1

To Emma
Who taught me everything I know
about the Brownie Guides

CHAPTER ONE

"Double Trouble"

The Wizlets loved a fight, and on the day that the Little Piddling Church Hall was double booked, they got one. It was the vicar's fault. He should never have poured that second glass of sherry while Akela was phoning to book the hall for the Scouts annual 5-a-side football tournament. The delicious anticipation of tasting that creamy, golden liquid made him completely forget that he'd already promised the hall to Brown Owl for the 4th Little Piddling Brownie

1

Guide Pack's First Aid practical. As a consequence, when both packs turned up at the same time and staked their claim to the hall, there was a helluva hullabaloo. The Scouts put up their goalposts and refused to take them down, while the Brownies laid their First Aid dummy in the middle of the hall and elastoplasted it to the floor. It was a stand-off. Brownies to the left, Scouts to the right, and in the middle, the full-fat figure of battling Brown Owl nose to nose with a livid Akela, a short, pear-shaped man in a pair of man-shaped shorts. Neither would give way. Pack honour was at stake. It was a military stalemate!

"Little Piddling Church Hall ain't big enough for the both of us!" sneered Brown Owl.

"Then we'll just have to play football around you," countered the weaselly tones of Akela.

"We'll use your players for bandage practice if you do," jeered Brown Owl. "We'll tie their legs together so they fall over!"

"Just listen to them," said Candy, who was sitting on the pack's red tin mushroom surrounded by the rest of the Trolls. "They sound like a pair of babies."

"Don't you dare say horrible things about our lovely leader," hissed The Honorable Tatiana Bortafue-Banks, who was using her waiting-time wisely to embroider a silk handkerchief that she'd bought for the dew drop on the end of Brown Owl's nose.

"She's magnificent and glorious," glowed Priscilla Pinch, adding, "I've just adopted a penguin and I've called it Brown Owl."

"Oh, congratty-tatties," giggled Tati. "She will be pleased."

"Oh, do put a sock in it," cried Big

George who, like the rest of the Trolls, felt sick when the Fairies toadied up to Brown Owl.

"Coming up," piped the voices of the two tiny brownie elves inside Raindrop Henderson's pocket, and with a wiggle of their button-noses they magicked a large steaming rugby sock out of the ether and lodged it in between Priscilla's teeth. The Scouts burst their breeches at the sight of Priscilla choking on a sweaty sock, while Priscilla started to cry.

"Quiet!" shouted Brown Owl, her fat face wobbling like the flanks of a walrus. "Akela and I can't hear ourselves bicker."

"Well I'm not going outside into the cold to do First Aid," whispered Anita. "I didn't bring a jumper."

"Can't you do something?" Raindrop Henderson asked the widdly wizards.

"I can tap dance," said Vac.

"To make the Scouts go outside," sighed Raindrop just a little too loudly. The Scouts overheard this remark and called the Brownie Guides rude names, like chocolate brownies and brown cowpats, while the two largest boys, Sebastian and Tarquin, told Raindrop that she'd better learn her First Aid good, because she'd need it after the Scouts had beaten her up. Raindrop wanted to cry, but Anita wouldn't let her.

"Don't show them that you're frightened," she said.

"I think we should rumble them," said Candy, flexing her Kung Fu kicking leg. Big George agreed.

"Yeah!" she growled. "Rumble them right up their backsides!"

"Plum duff 'em!" squeaked the two little voices from inside Raindrop's pocket. Anita giggled.

"That's a pudding, isn't it?" she said.

"A great big fat one," roared Vac, "just like Brown Owl!"

Shake popped his head over the edge of Raindrop's pocket and swore at his partner.

"You squeaky-clean scrubbing brush!" he shrieked. "How many times do I have to tell you NOT to shoot off spells without my permission?" Vac poked his head out to see what he'd done. Brown Owl had turned into a large stodgy plum pudding and was sitting steaming in the middle of the hall. The strange thing was that nobody

noticed. This was partly due to the fact that Brown Owl always looked like a pudding (without the holly on top, obviously), and partly due to the loud, hysterical screaming coming from the other side of the hall, where Sebastian and Tarquin were bending down, pretending to readjust their shoelaces, so that they could look up Tawny Owl's dress. Raindrop grabbed Shake and Vac and squeezed their waists.

"Chrome-cleaning mousse!" cursed Vac.

"Flannel-flicked faucets!" squealed Shake. "That hurts!"

"If you don't change Brown Owl back into a human being and send those rude Scouts outside, I'll squidge you like a tube of toothpaste," she threatened, as the panting pixies turned purple in the face.

"All-wiping-right!" gasped Shake. "You win!" Raindrop released her grip

and Vac turned the plum pudding back into Brown Owl with a blue-flamed flash of brandy fire. "And I'll cast a good manners spell to sort the Scouts out," said Shake. "Hand me the book of elfin magic, Vac. Now what do you think? Number 48?"

"49," said Vac, mischievously. "It's harder to get out of." So spell number 49 it was. MAKING BOYS BEHAVE LIKE GENTLEMEN.

"In the game of etiquette
The rules are clear and firmly set.
Boys must always take the pain
And play their football in the rain. . ."

Shake suddenly stopped chanting.

"Is that the end?" asked Raindrop.

"Bleached bog bowls!" he exploded. "The next page is missing. I can't finish it."

"I can," said Vac. "It's a piece of easy-peasy pumpkin pie!"

"...And play their football in the rain.
 So Cupid bend your golden bow
And melt the girlies' hearts like snow."

"Oh no, that's not right." But Vac had said it now. His misplaced magic spell was out of the bag. It floated across the room like fine mist and settled in the hair of the Fairies and Brown Owl, reprogramming them from sly, scheming sourpusses into ghastly, gooey-eyed lovers. Suddenly, Brown Owl saw Akela through rose-tinted spectacles. This squat little despot was the handsomest man she'd ever set eyes on, and Tati and Priscilla were limp with swoon-fever for the two bullies Sebastian and Tarquin.

"You dust-buster!" roared Shake, clipping his fellow elf around the ears. "Now look what you've done!"

"I think I said the Falling In Love spell by mistake," mumbled Vac, sheepishly.

"Can't you cancel it?" asked Candy.

Vac shook his head.

"It's one-way only," he apologized. And well might he have done, because his clumsy conjuring had condemned the Trolls to First Aid in the freezer. Brown Owl was being embarrassing, attending to Akela's every whim. There was nothing she wouldn't do for her beloved beau now. If he wanted the hall for his football, then the hall he should have. The Brownie Guides would happily retire outside into the jaws of the biting North wind.

"It's our pleasure," she simpered.

"Oh, absolutely," grinned the fluttering Fairies, batting their eyelashes at Sebastian and Tarquin.

"Whoops!" grinned Vac, cheesily, as Raindrop and the Trolls fixed him with a withering stare and marched outside to freeze their legs off. "It was an accident!"

Accident or not, at that precise moment in time, the Wizlets were considerably less popular than a floating rat in a camp-fire pot of ratatouille.

CHAPTER TWO

"Emergency Pow Wow"

It was colder than a penguin's lunch box outside the hall. The Brownie Guides sat and shivered underneath the stars. At least, the Trolls did. Brown Owl had borrowed Akela's fawn body-warmer and the Fairies had fluttered and puckered until Sebastian and Tarquin had lent them their thick woolly jumpers, which kept them warmer than hot buttered toast.

"Any questions?" asked Brown Owl, after she had demonstrated how to bandage the First Aid dummy from head to toe.

"Could I be the dummy?" shivered Anita. The bandages looked lovely and warm.

"Certainly not," snapped Brown Owl. "A little bit of frostbite never hurt anyone." Raindrop's hands were so cold she couldn't feel her fingertips as she raised her hand.

"Please, Brown Owl," she chattered through frozen lips, "I want to call an emergency pow-wow." A nervous hush fell over the 4th Little Piddling Brownie Guide Pack. Of course, every Brownie had the right to call an emergency pow-wow, in which the girls were allowed to make decisions without Brown Owl's help, but in Little Piddling no girl had dared to challenge the leader's authority for over one hundred years . . . (not since the infamous mutiny of 1864, when the then Brown Owl had been ducked in the pond to see if she was a witch or not) … which made Raindrop mucho macho! Brown Owl drew her lips tightly together, like a shrivelled prune, and glared at Raindrop.

"You insolent girl!" she barked.

"But I only want to suggest that our next venture should be a Sports Day against the Scouts," explained Raindrop. "It could be part of the village summer fête." The Trolls all nodded their heads.

"That's a great idea," said George. "We could beat them at running and teach them a lesson."

"And if we won, they'd stop pinching us and calling us names," added Candy.

The Fairies gasped and cried out, "No!"

"Sebastian will weep if he loses," explained Tati, breathlessly.

"And Tarquin will stop being gorgeous," added Priscilla, her cheeks

16

flushing pink at the mention of his name.

"I won't allow it!" ruled Brown Owl, striking a rosy vision of Akela's cute little hairless legs from her mind.

"Couldn't we take a vote on it?" persisted Raindrop.

"No," boomed Brown Owl. "Votes are for pow-wows and we're doing First Aid."

"I hate to say this," trembled the timid voice of Tawny Owl, "but technically we are in pow-wow, from the moment Raindrop called for it."

"Shut up!" steamed Brown Owl, who loved Akela more than Fudge Fingers and didn't want to upset him.

"So we really should take a vote," persisted Tawny Owl, bravely. The rule book had stranded Brown Owl up a gooey gum tree. She had to give in. The Trolls out-voted the Fairies by 4 to 2 and the Sports Day was confirmed.

While Brown Owl and the Fairies stomped back indoors to deliver the challenge to the Scouts, Shake and Vac jumped out of Raindrop's pocket and danced a jig on her head.

"You were fantabotastic!" they sang. "Can we help?"

"I was rather hoping you might," said Raindrop. "We're going to need all the magic you can muster to beat the boys."

"I agree," said Anita, doubtfully. "I know it's a good idea to teach those bad boys a lesson, but the Scouts have got much longer legs than us!"

"Speak for yourself," said George. Shake held up his hand for silence and pressed the bluebell megaphone to his lips.

"I know you're worried," he began, "but don't be. The Wizlets have all the answers. What you need is a lucky mascot."

"For what?" said Candy.

"For luck," said Shake. "And we suggest a goat."

"Yuck," said George. "They smell."

"Not if you wash them," said Vac. "Besides they've got nice deep pockets for sleeping in."

"A GOAT, you scum-shifting scourer!" roared Shake.

"Sorry," blushed Vac, "I thought you said coat."

"Why can't we have something more useful? Something that can run fast," asked Candy, "like a cheetah?"

"Because goats are the luckiest

creatures in Mishmash Major," said Shake indignantly. "That's the parallel world on the far side of nowhere where we come from, by the way. In Mishmash Major, the owning of a goat brings you better luck than touching a wooden black cat, curled up like a horseshoe, on a bed of purple heather, in the palm of the giant hand of a cosmic chimney sweep."

"And you lot are going to need luck by the lorry-load to beat the boys," chipped in Vac, cheerfully.

"Are you saying we're weedy?" bristled big-boned George.

"Yes," said Vac. Candy clenched her fist. "But I've just changed my mind."

"Listen," pleaded Shake. "Goats are good news. Trust us!" That was easier said than done, thought Raindrop, remembering the time at camp when they'd trusted Shake and Vac to build them a bivouac to sleep four, and they'd

built them a big anorak that only slept the top half of one.

There was a commotion in the doorway as Brown Owl stormed out of the hall with the furious Fairies in tow.

"They've accepted," she said sourly.

"But my Sebastian says he's going to beat you hollow," sneered Tati.

"So did my Tarquin," added Priscilla, competitively, "because he's just as fast! And don't expect us to help you."

"Because we won't," jeered Tati. "In fact we want to see you lose horribly!"

"Quite right," said Brown Owl. "I'm ashamed of you Trolls. The Scouts are boys, and as such are much better at running than you are. If you beat them, which I must say is most unlikely, you will scar them for life. You will humiliate them!"

"And they won't love us!" revealed Tati and Priscilla.

"Exactly!" boomed Brown Owl.

"Akela and the Scouts are our boyfri ...
I mean our good friends. If I had my way
I'd cancel this nonsense now, but you
'mutineers' appear to be in control." She
fixed Tawny Owl with a glowering stare
that turned her assistant's knees to jelly.
"No. You Trolls are on your own. If
you think you're better than the boys,
it's up to you to prove it!" What a
pompous brown cow she was, thought
Shake and Vac. It was high time some-
body told her what they thought of her.

"Brown Owl, you're foul!" they shrieked.

"Who said that?" spat the po-faced pack leader.

"I did," lied Raindrop, covering for the loud-mouthed imps. "I was just saying we should get a lucky mascot. A brown fowl might be nice."

"Or a goat," suggested George, cleverly.

"A goat!" snorted Brown Owl.

"Never!" But just then, fate played a hand, because Tatiana, rather liking the idea of a pack mascot, opened her mouth before her brain was in gear and blurted out.

"Ooh yes, a lucky mascot. That'd be lovely," which threw Brown Owl into a state of confusion. She couldn't veto a mascot if one of her beloved Fairies wanted one.

"Ah well, I never said we couldn't have a mascot," she said, changing her tune faster than a winded trumpeter. "But if the 4th Little Piddling Brownie Pack is to have a mascot it has to be suitable for young ladies."

"Something cuddly," suggested Priscilla, "like you, Brown Owl."

"Precisely my dear," beamed the flattered fattie.

"A hamster, or a pussy cat or a goldfish maybe?" suggested Tati.

"An excellent choice," said Brown Owl. The mystic midgets jumped up and down on Raindrop's head.

"No. It's got to be a goat," they cried, projecting their thoughts into Tawny Owl's head using magic mind control.

Whereupon Ms Mouse suddenly spoke up for the second time that night.

"May I suggest that each of the girls brings a pet in next week and we'll choose one of them to be our mascot?"

she said, by way of a compromise. Which is exactly what they decided to do, but not before Shake and Vac had conjured up two fairground shadows to box Brown Owl's ears until she agreed.

CHAPTER THREE

"Getting The Goat"

George's father worked on a farm and told the girls that if they could catch the billy goat, they could keep him as the pack mascot. The trouble is goats aren't easy to catch, especially when they think it's a game of touch tag. The Trolls ran around the paddock for three hours chasing the goat's tail, but every time they got close, it sprang away and laughed at them from its perch on top of the fence.

"This is hopeless," puffed Raindrop,

whose knees were covered in lumps and bumps from diving into thistles. The brownie elves were sunbathing lazily on top of a bale of hay, surveying the scene like Roman emperors.

"You'll never catch a goat with your hands," yawned Shake.

"You need a hammerfore," declared Vac.

"What's a hammerfore?" asked Anita.

"For banging in nails!" roared Vac, which reduced him and Shake to helpless giggles.

"Ha ha," said Raindrop, flatly. "Very funny. Thanks for your help."

"We're having a rest," protested Shake. "Making magic knocks the stuffing out of a brownie elf. Anyway, you're doing it all wrong. You need a goat trap."

"Oh no we don't," said Anita. "Not if it's another one of your jokes."

"No. A goat trap's real. You need a

wheelbarrow full of rotten cabbages, a few old rags, a tractor wheel and a snowstorm at just the right moment."

"Where are we going to get those?" asked George.

"Over there," said Vac, pointing to a pile of junk by the gate, which the girls were sent to fetch.

"Now what?" said Raindrop, after she'd rolled the tyre across the field like a giant Hula-Hoop.

"We attract the goat's attention," explained Shake. "Wave the rags, juggle

the cabbages and stand by to hurl the tyre like a frisbee," ordered Shake.

"So where does the snowstorm come in?" enquired Raindrop.

"That's just in case," winked Shake. "Now come on, get physical!"

But no matter how hard Anita waved, or Raindrop juggled, or Big George and Candy stood by with the rubber tyre, the goat just sat and stared at them as if they were soft in the head. After twenty minutes, the girls gave up.

"Our arms are aching," they moaned.

"Typical," tut-tutted Shake, turning upside down and standing on his hands. "I have to do everything around here." Then he stuck his floating toe into Vac's ear and incanted the words –

"Yo! No-flow snow go blow-ho!"

– a hundred times until they sounded

like gibberish. Lo and behold, a thick grey cloud, no bigger than an umbrella, gathered over the head of the goat and powdered it with snow. Shocked by this unexpected change in the weather, the goat bolted for the shelter of the hay rick. "Here it comes!" yelped the saucy sorcerers. "Wave your rags! Toss up those juicy cabbages! Stand by on the noose!" the goat was charging across the field, bucking its back legs and tossing its horns at the chasing snow cloud. Fifty metres, thirty metres, seventeen, eleven, six and a half. . . "Now tyre-girls, now!" But the tyre-girls were too tired and their feeble throw fell way short of the startled goat, causing it to veer sharply to the right, turn full circle and return to a lush spot of grass in the middle of the field, where it resumed lunch.

"Well, winkle out wax with a wet wipe," harrumphed Vac. "Don't you hopeless hu-women want to mash the

Scouts?" But before the goatless Trolls could answer, the air filled with laughter. The Trolls dropped the trappings of their trap and spun round to see Tati, Priscilla, Sebastian and Tarquin swinging on the farmer's gate.

"Brown Owl's going to be so cross with you," sneered Tati. "She said you couldn't have a goat."

"Yeah, and we're going to tell her what you're doing!" added Priscilla, hiding behind Tati in case George came after her. "And you're going to be in big – with a big B – trouble."

"Yeah," screamed Tati. "Such big – with a big B – trouble that she'll cancel the whole – with a big H – sports day!"

"We'll always be better than you!" jeered Sebastian and Tarquin, which made the Trolls madder than a bull on a barbecue. George was scarlet with rage, and Candy was itching to give them a switching.

"Ignore them," said Shake and Vac. "It's just words. Let's give them the cold shoulder." Then they re-directed the snow-cloud towards the gate and burst it over the Fairies' heads, shooting needles of freezing cold sleet down their backs. It was the Trolls' turn to laugh as Tati, Priscilla, Sebastian and Tarquin beat a wailing retreat pursued by a storm front.

"But we still haven't got a goat," pointed out Raindrop, when the last shriek had subsided, "and Brownies starts in half an hour, and you said that goats are the luckiest creatures in the parallel universe, and that in Mishmash Major, the owning of a goat brings you better luck than touching a wooden black cat, curled up like a horseshoe, on a bed of purple heather, in the palm of the giant hand of a cosmic chimney sweep. And that luck by the lorry-load was what we'd need to beat the boys."

"I know what I said," said Shake.

"That's because you said it," said Vac.

"So how are we going to get one?" interrupted Raindrop.

"By following my nose," said the instinctive imp, twitching his nostrils in the direction of a frightful pong.

The Wizlets sat on Raindrop's shoulder and directed her into a housing estate on the outskirts of Little Piddling. The Trolls scanned the streets for goats, but saw nothing but a lazy dustcart crashing and clanking its way towards the village school. The widdly wizards exchanged smug smiles.

"Can no one see the goat?" Shake asked. The Brownie Guides shook their heads. "The spell book, if you please," he said, holding out his hand.

"Why, certainly," puffed Vac. "FARM ANIMALS FROM EVERY-DAY KNICK-KNACKS, I presume?"

"Precisely," agreed Shake. "Number one thousand and three and a bit. Everybody ready?"

"For what?" exclaimed Raindrop, but Shake was already chanting, and thrusting his chin in and out like a clucking hen.

"Where there's muck
There is also a mickle.
Where there's grime,
There is also some gold.
Where there's rubbish and trash
And an unwanted stash,
There's a goat
To be grown out of mould!"

There was a flash of light, a puff of smoke and a ghostly bleating that seemed to come from everywhere and nowhere all at the same time. When the smoke cleared, the dustcart had vanished and standing in its place was a large billy goat, with a battered old teddy bear stuffed through the collar round its neck.

"It's a lucky goat!" exclaimed Raindrop. "Now we can win! You're brilliant!"

"You haven't seen what it can do yet," boasted Shake, mysteriously, as the goat tugged the teddy bear out of its collar and gobbled it up in one ginormous gulp.

CHAPTER FOUR

"A Beast of a Feast"

The lucky goat was a dustcart on legs, which proved to be rather unlucky for Little Piddling. On the way to the church hall it ate everything in its path. Hedgerows, front gardens, a policeman's bicycle, a shopping trolley, fourteen charity boxes, two pounds of bananas, a telephone box and three snappy, yappy dogs, which the Trolls were glad to see the back of. By the time they reached the church hall, the goat's stomach was bulging like Father Christmas's toy sack.

When the Trolls pushed open the hall doors, Brown Owl slipped from the shadows with a face as long as a clown's boot.

"You disobedient girls!" she raged. "I said no goats!" The Fairies, their hair towelled-dry after the snowstorm and each wearing a pair of Brown Owl's fluffy slippers, were sipping mugs of steaming cocoa behind their leader's broad back and smiling sneaky smiles.

"We thought you might change your mind when you met it," said Raindrop, meekly. Brown Owl's nostrils were an answer in themselves. They flared like two whales' blow holes.

"Take that filthy beast out of here," she seethed, "and don't come back till you've got proper pets to show." Proper pets like Tati's and Priscilla's, who between them had gone out and bought a gerbil, a rabbit, a singing cockatoo, a tankful of tropical fish, a chipmunk, a

tortoise and a Pekingese dog with a snotty snout.

"Well that's that then," said Raindrop glumly, as the Trolls regrouped outside.
  "Jumping J-cloths," fizzed Vac. "Where's your spirit? You can't give up now!"

"But she won't let us have the goat as our lucky mascot, and without our lucky mascot we can't beat the boys, and if we can't beat the boys they'll call us names and stuff for ever!"

Shake's eyes twinkled wickedly.

"You'll get your goat," he grinned, flicking through his instruction manual for some extra-special spells. "Ah, here we are. This one's well-wild and woolly!"

Five minutes later the Trolls re-entered the hall, to find Brown Owl petting Tati's bunny rabbit.

"The Fairies and I have chosen a pack mascot," she declared. "It's Fluffy."

"But you haven't seen *our* pets yet," piped up Candy.

"I've already told you," snapped Brown Owl. "I hate goats!"

"Not the goat. Our *other* pets," smiled Candy, opening the doors and ushering

in a procession of hungry wild animals. There was a wolf, a python, a tiger, an eagle, a monitor lizard and a swamp crocodile with a twin deck of snick-snacking teeth. Brown Owl screamed and jumped into Tati's arms, but Tati chose the same moment to jump into Priscilla's arms, who unfortunately was frozen stiff with fear and had her arms fixed rigidly by her sides. Brown Owl and Tati clashed in mid air like two hot air balloons, and bounced into Priscilla, knocking her to the ground like a wooden skittle. In the confusion of arms and legs, Fluffy hopped into the middle of the room, cocked his head at the strange, scaly monitor lizard, and was woofled up from behind by the wolf. This casual snack acted like a dinner bell. In a flurry of feathers and fur, the eagle silenced the cockatoo, the python chomped the chipmunk, the lizard guzzled the gerbil, the crocodile snapped

up the tortoise (and washed it down with gallon of goldfish), while the tiger tickled his tastebuds with the particularly piquant Pekingese dog, snotty snout and all. Then Shake and Vac sneezed simultaneously and the jungle beasts vanished back whence they'd come, with a yelp, a growl and a magical lick of their lips.

"Oh dear," dissembled Raindrop. "It looks like there's only one pet left." The Trolls covered their mouths to stifle their giggles, as the Fairies dripped hot tears and Brown Owl picked herself up off the floor.

"In that case," she trembled, still taken aback by the tiger's table manners, "I think we'd better have the goat as our mascot." Then she added, "That'll be all for today, girls," in a voice that cracked like splintered glass.

Round One to the Wizlets – lucky goat got, now for the scummy Scouts!

CHAPTER FIVE
"Thuggery And Skulduggery"

The village fête was the following Saturday. Brightly-coloured stalls popped up all over the green as the villagers prepared to go fête-crazy. A large section of open ground had been designated a tent-free zone, and an aged council worker was painstakingly painting a running track on to the grass, by touching up each individual blade with a pot of white enamel paint and a pygmy paint brush.

The Fairies had refused to run against

their boyfriends and Brown Owl, for the sake of Akela, had given them her full support. It was the Trolls, therefore, who turned up first at the meeting place, underneath the famous village tree known to all the local dogs as the Little Piddling Oak. Raindrop tied the goat (now called Gerald) to a branch and unpacked her sports gear.

"Everyone confident?" asked Vac.

"I should say so!" boomed George.

"We've got a lucky mascot," cheered Candy, rubbing Gerald's ears. "We can't lose!" A hollow laugh knocked Candy's optimism.

"Surely you mean, *can't win!*" roared Sebastian and Tarquin, who were sitting on a branch above the Trolls' heads, spying. The boys jumped to the ground and linked arms with the Fairies, who'd appeared round the side of the tree trunk. The four of them were glued together like slithering slugs in a jam jar and grinning at the Trolls in a superior sort of a way.

"We're the best," said the Scouts, "and don't you forget it!" George wanted to grind the smug smiles off their faces with an electrical sander, but just then Tawny Owl arrived with a trembling bottom lip and a plate of burnt scones for the cake stall. The Trolls made polite yum yum noises when asked if they'd like a taste.

"Not just now," declined Anita. "They look dis..." she stopped herself just in time. "Dis...licious though."

"You're just being nice," sniffed Tawny Owl. "I know I can't cook. I know they taste like lumps of coal!"

"Oh, but they don't," lied the Trolls kindly.

"Oh yes they do!" punched the strident voice of Brown Owl, a truth which reduced Tawny Owl to a howling, blubbering, nervous wreck. Brown Owl had been making cowy eyes at Akela over by the Hogroast. Now she was smiling a secret, golden-memory smile as she called the pack to order.

"Well," she said, placing her hands on her face to cool her flushed cheeks, "I can't say that I'm pleased to be here, but now that we are, it is our duty as Brownie Guides to uphold the reputation of the 4th Little Piddling Brownie Guide pack."

"Does that mean the Fairies will be racing too?" asked Raindrop.

"Certainly not," snapped Tati and Priscilla. "We're here to see that the Scouts win!" Brown Owl shot them a fierce look that told them to keep their mouths shut.

"Something's afoot!" hissed Shake into Raindrop's ear.

"Yes. Twelve inches," volunteered Vac.

"I mean," glowered his fellow elf, "that something's going down."

"A submarine?" queried Vac the Vacant. Shake booted him off Raindrop's shoulder and he slithered down her T-shirt.

"There's trouble brewing," he stated for the third time. "I can smell it!"

"It's probably Tawny Owl's scones," whispered Vac, as he heaved himself back on to Raindrop's shoulder by monkey-climbing her hair.

"Before the races, therefore," plotted Brown Owl, beaming like a hyena, "we shall be giving a First Aid demonstration over by the tea tent." Tati and Priscilla snorted like a pair of prissy pigs. Something was definitely afoot! "And the Trolls will be giving it," announced Brown Owl with a flourish.

"But we've got to warm up for Sports Day," protested Candy.

"Exactly," snickered Priscilla.

"Why can't the Fairies do it?" moaned George. "It's always us who get the boring jobs."

"I won't have any arguments," barked Brown Owl. "Tawny Owl will supervise and this goat will remain tethered to the Little Piddling Oak out of harm's way. Any questions?"

"Only one," thought Shake. "Why?"

That was obvious. While Raindrop, Candy, George and Anita tied themselves in knots and demonstrated kissing, bandaging and plastering to a group of uninterested adults, Brown Owl, the Fairies, Sebastian and Tarquin nobbled the Trolls' sports equipment. They stitched up their sacks for the sack race; they bent their spoons for the egg and spoon; they cut their rope for the three-legged sprint; and worst of all, they buried their running shorts, so that the Trolls would have to compete in their pants, an embarrassment that would guarantee the Scouts a victory in every event.

Fortunately for the unsuspecting Trolls, sorcery and a goat were at hand. Gerald alerted Shake and Vac to the cheating by bleating loudly. The brownie elves flew over to see what was going down and blew a gasket.

"Fer...licking feather dusters!" Vac exploded.

"Vanishing grease spots!" thundered Shake. "She's slipping slippy worms into the Trolls' shoes. They'll be sliding all over the place! We'll get her for this," and they made up a socking great spell on the spot to pay Brown Owl back for being such a skulduggerer!

"Dirty doers of the cheaty kind
Need a butt up their behind."

The magic sent Gerald Geronimo-crazy. He gnawed through his rope and bounced free of the Little Piddling Oak, delivering a well-timed head butt to

Brown Owl's ballooning bottom and scattering her cowardly accomplices to the four corners of the village green. Brown Owl flapped her arms like a flying squid as she hurtled through the air and splatted head first into a lemon meringue pie, which promptly disappeared down her gob. Shake and Vac dusted off their hands.

"That'll teach the old swindler!" declared Shake.

"Congratulations, Gerald. You can come back now." But Gerald was trotting round the fête looking for something to eat.

"Oh dear," grimaced Shake, as Gerald guzzled Mr Fallowbottom's prize-winning giant marrow.

"Let's whistle tunelessly and make like we don't know him," suggested Vac.

"Good idea," said Shake, looking up at the clouds and pretending to count them. Meanwhile Gerald was having the time of his life. He dribbled in the home-made jam; he guessed the weight of the cake by putting it in his mouth; he ripped up the Punch and Judy man's tent, leaving a trail of striped rags across the grass; he chewed through the hose-pipes on the new Little Piddling fire engine; he scoffed all of the food for the barbecue (which was abandoned as a result of having no bangers and no burgers to go in no buns); and he polished off the second-hand clothes on the jumble sale stall. The only things he didn't eat were Tawny Owl's scones, which he found rather hard to swallow. As you might expect, when Tawny Owl discovered this she was inconsolable for a week.

Gerald ran amok. The fête was turned upside down. When the organizers finally caught him they were furious, and wanted to know why the Brownie Guides had been allowed to bring a goat. Needless to say, Brown Owl blamed the Trolls, and the four girls were forced to clean up the mess all on their own, while the newly-painted track was cleared for the races and Gerald was locked away in the Public Address caravan.

"I thought you said a goat was lucky!" hissed Raindrop, as the Trolls trudged back to the Little Piddling Oak after tidying the village green. The halfpint pixies smiled cheesily.

"I think he was hungry," said Vac.

"Has anyone seen my shorts?" shouted Candy, out of the blue. The sabotage was as yet undetected.

"Well, I fail to see how Gerald can bring us luck from inside that caravan," stated George, gloomily.

"Don't worry," said Shake encouragingly. "You've got Vac and me now!" The girls groaned. The mystic midgets' hit and miss magic was hardly a substitute for a lucky mascot. Out on the track, there was a whine as the starter switched on his battery-operated megaphone.

"Good afternoon, ladies and gentlemen, welcome to the Scouts versus Brownie Guides Sports DAAAYYY!"

The megaphone howled like a dog with its paw stuck in the fridge.

"I've lost my shorts too," exclaimed Raindrop.

"And me!" panicked Anita.

"All our shorts have disappeared!" wailed George. "I'll never find another pair in my size."

"So what do we do now?" Raindrop demanded crossly of the brownie elves. "We can't run in our pants. It's rude!" Shake looked pensive.

"I'm thinking," he said.

"Well, you'd better think faster," snapped Raindrop. "They're calling us for the sack race. Oh oh! Look out, here comes trouble!"

"Problem?" sniggered Tati, pointing to the Trolls' lack of shorts. "It looks like the Super Scouts have already beaten the pants off you!"

"Take a hike!" said Big George. "Or I'll hook you up in this tree."

"Oooh, scary!" mocked Priscilla. "I don't think! Come on Tati, let's go and watch our boyfriends win."

"I've got it,' yelped Shake, as the Fairies skipped off into the crowd. "Bring me those rags from the Punch and Judy stall." He flicked through the spell book, mumbling, "Sewing, sewing, sewing... Ah, here it is. Right, quick! The four of you stand by to be patched up."

*"If it's true that rags make riches
Turn these rags into some breeches!"*

Something glinted in the sunshine. In the twinkle of a needle's eye, each of the Trolls found herself dressed in a pair of stripy short trousers. Shake beamed like a parcels-only letter box.

"Now go out there and win!" he cheered, as the girls picked up their sacks and rushed on to the track, leaving Vac looking most put out.

"Huh!" he muttered. "Hit and miss magic indeed! The cheek of it."

The starter grunted disapprovingly as the Trolls arrived at the starting line. He had a christening to attend and wanted to hurry things along.

"Sorry we're late," they gasped. "We're ready now."

"About time too," he snapped sourly. "On your marks, get set..."

Raindrop screamed. The Trolls weren't set at all. Their sacks wouldn't open!

"Bad Sports"

As the starter's finger twitched and curled around the pistol's trigger, the Wizlets gulped. The Scouts crouched tensely in their sacks ready to leap forward, while Brown Owl puckered her lips at Akela and blew him a pre-victory kiss.

"Don't panic!" hollered Shake and Vac to the Trolls. "Just unpick your sacks while we try to stall the Scouts." A puff of smoke drifted lazily across the green as the starting pistol cracked. The

boys were off, the girls were still franti-
cally stitch-picking and Shake was
searching madly for a spell.

"Got it!"

"Furry friends with poisoned fang,
Spin your webs to trap this gang!"

– he cried, and all of a sudden the boys
stopped hopping, and started whooping
and whirling and screaming blue murder
instead. They rolled on the floor and
kicked off their sacks in a flapping, flat
panic.

"Help!" they shrieked, as the Trolls
snipped through the Fairies' fat stitches
and opened their sacks.

"There's a creepy-crawly down my
shorts!" bawled Tarquin. Vac fluttered
over to the Brownie Guides and urged
them to hurry.

"Now's your chance to stuff 'em!" he
roared, as the boys scrambled out of their

sacks, which were bulging with balls of seething, scuttling, spitting, spinning, hairy-shanked spiders, and the Trolls bounced down the empty track to victory.

While the crowd applauded, Brown Owl and the Fairies smiled weakly at their loved ones, but their fluttering, dewy-eyed looks were not returned. Akela felt betrayed and was stony-faced in defeat, while Sebastian and Tarquin still had spiders on the brain.

"Ooh, ooh, ooh, I say!" exclaimed Brown Owl suddenly, as if she had a hot potato in her mouth. "It's the egg and spoon race next!" The thought of this cheered her up no end, and she sniggered up her sleeve as she remembered what a mess they'd made of the Trolls' spoons.

They were twisted like tree roots, corkscrewed so far out of shape that the Trolls had to contort their bodies like pipe cleaners to balance their eggs.

"We can't run like this," protested George. The only way to keep the egg on her spoon was to tuck both arms through her legs and shuffle backwards like a camel.

"Then walk," suggested Vac.

"How can we win if we walk?" flustered Candy, who was bent double in the crab position.

"That's our problem," grinned the wee-widdly wizards, burying their heads in their elfin spell book and warming to their roles as Master Mischief-Makers!

When the Scouts first saw the Brownies' buckled spoons they fell over laughing, which made the starter rather anxious. If he didn't get away soon, he'd miss the bath bit in the font! He clicked his fingers and chivvied the hysterical boys back on to their feet.

"Ready?" he shouted, barely pausing before he added, "Get on with it." The Scouts sprinted into a comfortable lead while the girls crept forward like four arthritic tortoises. But halfway down the track, the Scouts' eggs suddenly started growing. In under a second they were thirty times their original size and weighed only slightly less than a baby elephant. The Scouts came to a grinding halt. The eggs rolled off their spoons, cracked when they hit the ground and started to hatch. Only they weren't chickens that emerged from the shells. They were dinosaurs – vicious, razor-toothed Raptors, whose only pleasure in

life was to chase Boy Scouts all over the village green and snap at the seat of their shorts. Shake and Vac danced a jig on the groundsman's heavy roller as the Brownie Guides finished first, second, third and fourth, taking maximum points. Brown Owl and the Fairies buried their heads in their hands and wondered how it could be that their

best-laid plans were going so woefully wrong.

It got worse. When the Trolls discovered that their ropes for the three-legged race had been cut in half, Shake and Vac came to the rescue by giving each of them a third leg so they could run individually.

> *"Wooden pin*
> *And wooden peg*
> *Conjure up*
> *A middle leg."*

The Trolls were run-away victors. In fact, with three legs apiece, they ran away so fast that they all made it into the tea tent before the boys had even finished.

The Scouts were livid. The crowd had started to cheer the Brownies and to greet the sulks and tantrums of the boys with cold silence.

"Your girls are making us look like fools," Akela complained to Brown Owl.

"I thought you said you were going to help us win," moaned Sebastian and Tarquin bitterly to the Fairies.

"We're doing our best," snapped Tati. "It's not our fault that you run like aged old warthogs!" Priscilla nodded her head.

"You never told us you had two left feet," she said. The boys huffed and puffed and said they could never love liars, which made the Fairies cry and Brown Owl all protective and mumsy.

"There, there," she comforted, "If I told you I had a plan to beat all plans, that will scupper the Trolls once and for all, would that make you feel better?"

"You bet," cheered Tati and Priscilla, turning off the waterworks faster than a plumber. "Have you?"

"Well no," replied Brown Owl, "but I'm working on it."

CHAPTER SEVEN

"Dib, dib dib!
Sob, sob, sob!"

When Brown Owl finally came up with a plan to trounce the Trolls it was a stinker. As the next event was the Tug of War, she was going to hammer nails through the soles of the boys' plimsolls to give them extra grip, and to smear the bottom of the Trolls' trainers with butter so they'd slip, slide and slither their way to mud-splattered defeat. What Brown Owl didn't know was that Shake and Vac were floating above her head on a dandelion puff, eavesdropping on every word she said.

"Whiter-than-white washing pow-ders!" exclaimed Vac. "She's a scrub-a-dub monster."

"Abso-Loo-Blue-lutely!" agreed Shake. "We'd better do something quick!" So they flapped their arms to steer their puffball down to earth and scampered over to the Trolls to tell them what was what.

"This time they've gone too far," professed Raindrop. "I vote we put them out of action once and for all."

"But how?" said Anita.

"We could get Gerald to eat them," suggested Candy.

"Or I could sit on them," offered Big George.

"But we need you," Raindrop reminded her. "You're our Tug of War anchorgirl."

"First Aid!" squealed Vac suddenly, leaping to his feet and clipping Shake around the ear in his excitement.

"But they're not injured," said a puzzled Anita.

"They would be if I Kung-Fued them," growled Candy.

"No. We tie them up with bandages," explained Vac. "We wrap them up like Egyptian mummies till the races are over!"

Everyone agreed it was a brilliant plan, which made Vac's head swell to three times its normal size. "They don't call me Einstein for nothing," he bragged.

"They don't call you Einstein at all," scoffed Shake, bashing Vac's empty head by way of a payback and starting a furious elfin fist-fight, which lasted for several bruising minutes and wasted precious mummy-wrapping time.

By the time the Trolls had separated the two pugilistic pixies, the Scouts were shod in their illegal, spiked plims and

Brown Owl and the Fairies were ordering the Trolls to lie down on their backs for a trainer inspection. The Trolls refused, knowing what they knew about the buttering plot, but Brown Owl reminded them sternly that it was a Brownie Guide's duty to obey Brownie Guide Law at all costs, and that if they'd bothered to read their Brownie Guide handbook they'd know that the Brownie Guide Promise required them to do Brown Owl's bidding at all times! What a dilemma. On the one hand, the Trolls knew that if they lay down their trainers would be greased and they'd lose the Tug of War. On the other hand, Brown Owl looked so fierce that to refuse her order was bound to end in tears. And on the third hand, the starter was biting his nails and hopping up and down on the spot, desperate to get the tugging underway in case the christening started without him. He *was* the vicar after all!

What should the poor girls do?

Fortunately, that decision was taken by the Wizlets, with the help of a deadly dollop of mystical, Middle-Eastern magic. Vac produced a Snake Charmer's flute from behind his ear and whistled a tune that so entranced the First Aid bandages that they unravelled and wound themselves around the legs of Brown Owl and the Fairies. In no time at all the pack leader and her pets were trussed up tighter than flies in a spider's web, their cries muffled by corn plasters. "Right," said Vac. "That's it. You won't hear another peep out of them all afternoon, which leaves you lot free to rout the Scouts."

Which is exactly what happened. There was a tiny hiccup on the first pull of the Tug of War, when the Trolls slid rather quickly to defeat, but that was because of the Scouts' spiked plims.

Shake and Vac swiftly put matters right on the second pull, by casting an invisibility spell on Big George. The Scouts were twice as cocky, thinking they only had to pull against three girls, but as they took up the strain, invisible George tickled their armpits, which made them drop the rope and fall backwards on to their bottoms. From then on the Scouts never got a look in. They lost the deciding tug flat on their faces in the mud. Then they lost the High Jump, because Shake and Vac put magnets into their trainers and every time they jumped, the magnets dragged the bar off. They failed miserably at the long jump, because the run-up track mysteriously turned to treacle whenever it was one of their turns, and tossing the welly proved to be a living nightmare for Sebastian and Tarquin. In mid throw, the wee-widdly wizards turned the boys' wellies into boomerangs. No matter how far they threw them, they always came back, and the boys ended up with the suicidally sad scores of minus four and minus five metres respectively.

The Brownie Guides won every event by a mile and a half and were presented with a large silver cup. The Scouts lost their sense of humour and slunk away with their tails between their legs. When Tawny Owl untied Brown Owl and the Fairies, the three schemers burst into floods of self-pitying tears,

because Akela, Sebastian and Tarquin wanted nothing more to do with them. Their foolish, corrupting love had withered on the vine.

"There's still one thing I don't understand," Raindrop said to Shake and Vac, as the Trolls enjoyed a victory lap of honour in front of the cheering crowd. "Gerald's been locked in that caravan all afternoon, yet we still won everything. We didn't need him as a lucky mascot at all." The saucy sorcerers chuckled with glee.

"We lied about the goat!" they said. "A goat's no luckier than an earthworm or a mosquito."

"So why did you make us get one?" asked Candy.

"Because once you'd got him, you believed that you could win," chuckled Shake, blowing the lock on the caravan door with a crackling spark of finger lightning.

"Which means Gerald's just an ordinary goat?" clarified Raindrop, as Gerald leapt across the grass towards a blubbing, broken-hearted Brown Owl and the snivelling, forlorn Fairies.

"Buffed-up bedpans, no!" roared Vac. "There's nothing ordinary about Gerald. He's one of us."

"One of you?" puzzled George.

"He's a goblin from Mishmash Major," explained Shake. "*Trouble* is his middle name."

"Oh dear," muttered Raindrop. "I don't like the sound of that. Where is he now?"

"Over there," snickered Shake and Vac. "Now that's what we call funny!" They pointed to the other side of the green, where the goblin goat was gobbling two brown and yellow uniforms and a very large, blue one. In the distance, three half-naked figures scampered down the High Street, picking up their fleshy knees and running for all they were worth. It was Brown Owl, Tatiana and Priscilla, blushing to the frills on their baggy, brown pants!

The Trolls just had to laugh.

Oh, by the way, the goblin goat was adopted by Little Piddling as a lucky mascot. The village dustcart had mysteriously gone missing the week before, but Gerald proved to be so efficient at consuming black sacks and their contents that the dustcart was soon forgotten, and Gerald became as indispensable a part of the village as Mr Packet the postmaster, and Mr Snake and Mr Vic, two mysterious little men who took over the running of the Scouts for a while and taught them some long-overdue manners.